*To Brian, Jan, Chris and Tim*
*with many thanks*

**Illustrated by John Bianchi**
**Written by John Bianchi**
**© Copyright 1989 by Bungalo Books**

**Sixth printing 1997**

**Cataloguing in Publication Data**

Bianchi, John
  Champions of Hockey

ISBN 0-921285-18-3 (bound)    ISBN 0-921285-16-7 (pbk.)

I. Title.    II. Title: The Bungalo Boys III

PS8553.I26C53 1989    jC813'.54    C89-094143-2
PZ7.B526Ch 1989

Published in Canada by:          Trade Distribution:
Bungalo Books                    Firefly Books Ltd.
Ste.100                          3680 Victoria Park Ave.
17 Elk Court                     Willowdale, Ontario
Kingston, Ontario                M2H 3K1
K7M 7A4

Co-published in U.S.A. by:       Printed in Canada by:
Firefly Books (U.S.) Inc.        Friesen Printers
Ellicott Station                 Altona, Manitoba
P.O. Box 1338                    ROG OBO
Buffalo, New York
14205

Visit Bungalo Books on the Net at:
*www.bungalobooks.com*

Send E-mail to Bungalo Books at:
*Bungalo@cgocable.net*

# The Bungalo Boys III

*By John Bianchi*

## Champions of HOCKEY

The swoosh of steel on ice. The clatter of stick and puck. Sounds that crackle through frosted morning air. Sounds of the Bungalo Boys preparing for competition — a contest of skill, strength, grace and pluck. Sounds of hockey — the world's fastest game!

At stake is the symbol of hockey supremacy—the Bungalo Birdbath, installed by Great-Great-Granduncle Guido de Bungalo in 1889. Family tradition plays a big part in all Birdbath games. For 99 years, the Bath has been successfully defended against all challengers by the Bungalo sports dynasty. Indeed, many feel that the ghosts of these great hockey legends haunt the beaver pond to this very day.

This year's challengers are a mystery team from the Natural Hockey League. As player-coach Ma Bungalo puts her boys through their pregame skate, anxious eyes search the visitors' end of the ice. Finally, three small figures appear.

"It's a bunch of penguins!" laughs Curly. The rest of the boys cannot resist a moment of mirth. But their laughter is short-lived. Out of the morning haze, like three great ocean tankers clearing a fog, lumbers the rest of the NHL's team . . .

. . . the Bruins.

The icy determination that once flowed through the boys' veins quickly turns to Zamboni slush.

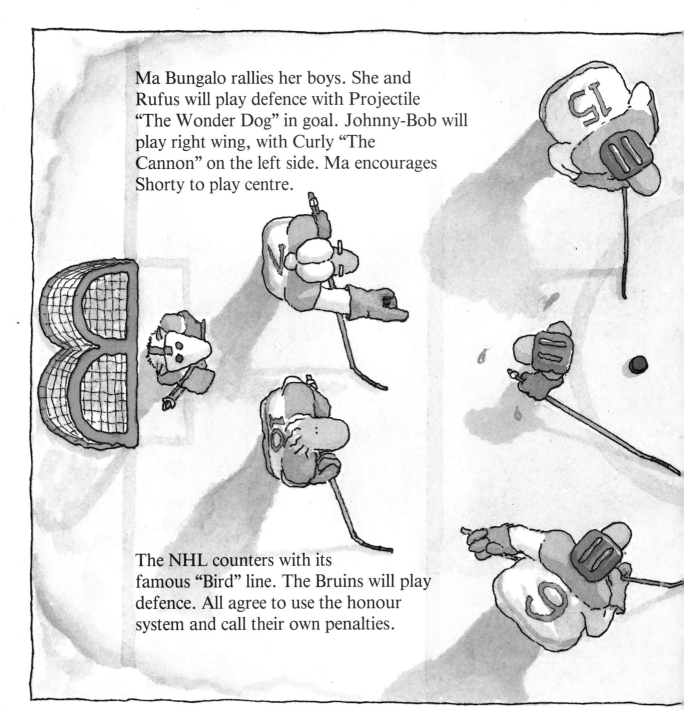

Ma Bungalo rallies her boys. She and
Rufus will play defence with Projectile
"The Wonder Dog" in goal. Johnny-Bob will
play right wing, with Curly "The
Cannon" on the left side. Ma encourages
Shorty to play centre.

The NHL counters with its
famous "Bird" line. The Bruins will play
defence. All agree to use the honour
system and call their own penalties.

The boys get off to a slow start. Little Shorty plays giveaway in his own end, and one of the big Bruin defencebears easily converts the miscue. NHL: one. Bungalos: no score.

Then, after going down to block a shot,
Little Shorty coughs up the puck.
Projectile is helpless as one of the Penguins
wastes no time turning on the red light.
NHL: two. Bungalos: no score.

Midway through the second period, Little Shorty takes a costly penalty and quickly sends himself to the penalty box. Inspired by the loss of their little centre, the Bungalos capitalize on their one-man disadvantage and score two unanswered goals. NHL: two. Bungalos: two.

In the third period, the NHL launches an all-out attack. The team pulls its big bruin goalie and fore-checks the Bungalos into their own end. The beaver pond has never seen such heavy action!

Suddenly, with a sickening **"CA-SPLASH,"** the ice shatters!

Out of the mayhem drifts a lone skater with the puck.
Little Shorty has a breakaway!

With time running out on the clock and his brothers offering words of encouragement, Little Shorty stickhandles toward the NHL's empty net. Some fans start a wave. The organist plays. Guided by the legendary Bungalo ghosts, Little Shorty takes careful aim.

He shoots . . .

During the post-game celebrations, the Bungalo Boys
congratulate each other on a game well played.
"We're still number one!" roars Curly.
"We never gave up!" shouts Johnny-Bob.
"We just did what we had to do!" cries Rufus.
"It was 60 minutes of teamwork," notes Ma.
**"Cause we're the Champions of Hockey**!" they all scream.
"And best of all," adds Little Shorty with relief,
"no one got into a fight."